KINTARO'S ADVENTURES
and Other
Japanese Children's Stories

KINTARO'S ADVENTURES
and Other
Japanese Children's Stories

edited by

Florence Sakade

illustrated by

Yoshio Hayashi

CHARLES E. TUTTLE COMPANY
Rutland, Vermont   *Tokyo, Japan*

Published by the Charles E. Tuttle Company, Inc.
of Rutland, Vermont & Tokyo, Japan
with editorial offices at Suido 1-chome, 2–6, Bunkyo-ku, Tokyo

International Standard Book No. 0–8048–0343–9

First edition, 1958
Twenty-ninth printing, 1989

PRINTED IN JAPAN

Stories in This Book

Publisher's Foreword

In 1952 we published the first edition of *Japanese Children's Stories from Silver Bells*, one of Japan's leading children's magazines. Since then, although the magazine is no longer published, the book has been so popular that successive reprintings have worn the plates past further use, and still orders pour in for it. To meet this continuing demand, we have now issued a revised edition of the book with entirely new illustrations and several new stories, in a single volume entitled *Japanese Children's Stories*, and also in two companion volumes entitled *Urashima Taro* and *Kintaro's Adventures*. We are confident these books will meet the same enthusiastic response as did the first edition.

A child who has been given a feeling of sympathy for the children of another country is on the way to becoming a true world citizen. For that reason those stories have been chosen with Japanese backgrounds which will both give the Western child a sense of identity with Japanese children and also explain some of the different customs. Indeed, it is this Japanese flavor which makes the stories appeal to older children at the same time as the stories remain simple enough for young children. And the illustrations are noteworthy for their Japanese flavor, serving as an introduction to the remarkable talent the Japanese artist has always possessed in the realms of line, color, and form.

Most of the stories are retellings of traditional Japanese stories, beloved through many generations, similar to those introduced to the English-speaking world by Lafcadio Hearn. But only in the case of "Urashima Taro" has a new version of one of Hearn's renderings been included, and that only because the story is too delightful to be omitted. To make the selection as representative as possible two modern stories have been included, "The Dragon's Tears" and "Why the Red Elf Cried," as well as a completely modern version of a famed classic, "Kintaro's Adventures," all by some of Japan's foremost contemporary storytellers.

Editorial responsibility for the book has been borne by Florence Sakade; both as a mother and as an editor and author of numerous children's publications, she has had wide experience in the entertainment and education of children. The English versions are the work of Meredith Weatherby, well-known translator of Japanese literature.

The Rolling Rice-Cakes

ONCE upon a time there was an old man and his old wife. One day the old man said: "I'm going to cut some firewood today. Please make me some rice-cakes for my lunch." So the old woman made rice-cakes and put them in the old man's lunch box. Then the old man left the house.

He went far into the forest and cut firewood all morning. When it was noon, he sat down to eat and opened his lunch box, saying: "Now, for some of the old lady's delicious rice-cakes."

Then he suddenly cried: "Oh, my!" because one of the rice-cakes had fallen out of the box, and he saw it go rolling away. Away it rolled, and suddenly down it plopped into a hole in the ground.

The old man ran over to the hole and—what do you know!—he could hear tiny voices singing inside the hole. "What's going on down there?" he asked himself. "I'll drop one more rice-cake down and see."

After he had dropped the second rice-cake into the hole, he put his ear close to the ground, and now he could hear the words of the song. And this is the song the tiny voices were singing:

> *Rice-cakes, rice-cakes,*
> *Nice, fat rice-cakes,*
> *Rolling, rolling, rolling—down!*

"What a beautiful song," the old man said, and he kept rolling rice-cakes down the hole until they were all gone. Then he leaned far over to peek into the hole.

Suddenly he called out: "Help! Help!" But it was too late—he had fallen in, and with a thump-thump-thump he too went rolling right down the hole.

There at the bottom of the hole he found hundreds of field mice. They had eaten all his rice-cakes and now they were singing again as they pounded rice.

"Thank you very much for the delicious rice-cakes, old man," the leader of the mice said. "To show our thanks we'll give you this bag of rice." And the mouse gave the old man a small bag of rice about the size of a fat coin purse.

"Goodbye, old rolling man," all the mice called. And then they sang another song:

> *Nice man, rice man,*
> *Nice, fat, mice man,*
> *Rolling, rolling, rolling—up!*

And as they sang the old man felt himself rolling right up and out of the hole.

Once he was on top of the ground, the old man brushed himself off and then went home, carrying the small bag of rice with him.

When his old wife heard his story and saw the rice, she said: "Humpf! That won't make more than two or three rice-cakes." But when she started pouring the rice out, they were surprised to discover that the bag always stayed full, no matter how much they poured out of it. It was a magic rice bag, a wonderful present that the mice had given them. After that they always had all the rice they could possibly eat. The old woman made rice-cakes for herself and the old man every day—mountains of them—and they lived happily ever afterward.

How to Fool a Cat

ONCE upon a time there was a rich lord who liked to collect carvings of animals. He had many kinds, but he had no carved mouse. So he called two skilled carvers to him and said:

"I want each of you to carve a mouse for me. I want them to be so lifelike that my cat will think they're real mice and pounce on them. We'll put them down together and see which mouse the cat pounces on first. To the carver of that mouse I'll give this bag of gold."

So the two carvers went back to their homes and set to work. After a time they came back. One had carved a wonderful mouse out of wood. It was so well done that it looked exactly like a mouse. The other, however, had done very badly. He had used some material that flaked and looked funny; it didn't look like a mouse at all.

"What's this?" said the lord. "This wooden mouse is a marvelous piece of carving, but this other mouse—if it is indeed supposed to be a mouse—wouldn't fool anyone, let alone a cat."

"Let the cat be brought in," said the second carver. "The cat can decide which is the better mouse."

The lord thought this was rather silly, but he ordered the cat to be brought in. No sooner had it come into the room than it pounced upon the badly carved mouse and paid no attention at all to the one that was carved so well.

There was nothing for the lord to do but give the gold to the unskillful carver, but as he did so he said: "Well, now that you have the gold, tell me how you did it?"

"It was easy, my lord," said the man. "I didn't carve my mouse from wood. I carved it from dried fish. That's why the cat pounced upon it so swiftly."

When the lord heard how the cat and everyone else had been fooled, he could not help laughing, and soon everyone in the entire court was holding his sides with laughter.

Well," said the lord finally, "then I'll have to give two bags of gold. One to the workman who carved so well, and one to you who carved so cleverly. I'll keep the wooden mouse, and we'll let the cat have the other one."

The Princess and the Herdboy

THIS is a tale of long and long ago, when the King of the Sky was still busy making stars to hang in the heavens at night. The king had a very beautiful daughter. She was called Weaving Princess because she sat at her loom all day long every day. She wove the most delicate stuff in the world. It was so light and airy, so thin and smooth, that it was hung among the stars in the sky and draped down toward the earth. It was the cloth that we now call clouds and fog and mist.

The King of the Sky was very proud of his daughter because she could weave so beautifully and was such a help to him. He was very busy making the sky, you see, and needed all the help he could get. But one day he noticed that Weaving Princess was becoming pale.

"Well, well, my little princess," the king said, "you've been working too hard I fear. So tomorrow you must take a holiday. Go out and play among the stars all day long. Then please hurry back and help me. I still need much more mist and fog, and many more clouds."

The princess was very happy to have a holiday. She'd always wanted to go and wade in the stream, called the Milky Way, that flowed through the sky. But she'd never had time before.

She put on her prettiest clothes and ran out among the stars, right over to the Milky Way. And there, in the middle of the stream, she saw a handsome boy, washing a cow in the water.

"Hello," the boy said to the princess, "who are you?"

"I'm the star Vega," she answered. "But everyone calls me Weaving Princess."

"I'm the star Altair," said the boy. "But everyone calls me Herdboy because I tend the cows that belong to the King of the Sky. I live over there on the other side of the Milky Way. Won't you come over to my house and play with me?"

So the herdboy put the princess on the back of the cow and led her across the stream to his house. They played all sorts of wonderful games and had so much fun that the princess forgot all about going home to help her father.

The King of the Sky became very worried when the princess failed to come home. He sent a magpie as his messenger to find her and tell her to come home. But when the magpie spoke to the princess she was having

such fun that she wouldn't even listen. Finally the king had to go himself and bring the princess home.

"You've been a very bad girl," the king said. "Just look at the sky—not even finished yet. You've been away playing and the sky needs clouds and mist and fog. So you can never have another holiday. You must stay here and weave all the time."

Then the king poured more and more star water into the Milky Way. Until now it had been a shallow stream that you could wade across, but the king poured in so much star water that it became a deep, deep river. The princess and the herdboy lived on opposite sides of the river, so now there was no way they could get across to each other.

So the princess went into her little house in the sky and sat in front of her loom. But she was so lonely and longed so much for Herdboy that she couldn't weave at all. Instead she just sat there weeping all the time. And the sky became emptier and emptier, with no clouds, and no mist, and no fog.

Finally the king said: "Please, my little princess, you mustn't cry all the time. I really need clouds and fog and mist for my sky. I tell you what I'll do. If you'll weave again and work hard, I'll let you go and play with the herdboy one day each year."

The princess was so happy when she heard this that she went right to work, and she's been working very hard ever since.

But once each year, on the seventh night of the seventh month, the King of the Sky keeps his promise to Weaving Princess. He sends a flock of magpies to the Milky Way, and with their wings they make a bridge

across the deep river. Then the princess goes running across the bridge of magpies to where the herdboy is waiting for her. And they have wonderful fun playing together for one whole night and one whole day.

And that's the reason why Japanese children celebrate a holiday called Tanabata-sama, "The Seventh Night of the Seventh Month." Children everywhere love to play and it makes them happy to know the Princess and Herdboy stars are having such fun together there up in the sky. So the children on earth decorate bamboo branches with bright pieces of paper and wave them in the sky, to remind the King of the Sky that it's time for him to keep his promise again.

Saburo the Eel-Catcher

ONCE there was a man named Saburo who was a famous eel-catcher. He was so expert that eels just couldn't resist his hook and so he always caught a lot of them. And when he caught one, he'd run right home and put it on the fire. Then when it was done, he would take it off the fire, put it on his rice, and eat it up, smacking his lips all the while. He thought that eels were delicious.

One day when he was fishing he felt a great pull on his line. "Oh, this one must be enormous!" said Saburo to himself as he pulled back with all his might. "Yo, heave, ho!" he shouted, and pulled out of the water just about the biggest eel that he had ever seen. "What an enormous eel!" cried Saburo, as the eel flashed out of the water. But he was pulling so hard that the eel flew right over his head and landed, with a big grunt, in the field behind him.

"Funny," said Saburo to himself as he looked for the eel. "Eels can't grunt. At least I don't think they can. Now, let's see. Where could he have gone to?" And Saburo began looking around the trees, in the tall grass, and under the big stones. But he couldn't find the eel anywhere. "Odd," he said, scratching his head. "I guess I pulled too hard and he went flying over the mountain." He kept on looking and suddenly saw

something big and long and black under a bush. "Aha," said Saburo rushing at it. But when he got there, he found it was only a big, black stick and no eel at all. "I never knew sticks and eels looked so much alike," he said, scratching his head.

Just then he saw a wild boar asleep in the grass. "Oh, my, I'd better be careful: wild boars are pretty dangerous." So he began tiptoeing around the sleeping boar, when all of a sudden he tripped over a stone and fell down with a thud. "Oh, that's done it!" said Saburo, trembling. The boar didn't move, though ordinarily the noise would have been enough to bring him charging through the grass at poor Saburo. So Saburo walked closer and saw the eel lying on top of the boar.

The boar was lying very still on its side, and the eel was sort of coiled on top with his head hanging over the boar's shoulder. "Oh, that's nice," said Saburo. "They've gone and made friends with each other. But I never knew eels and boars were friends before." But then he looked more closely and saw that the eel and the boar were both quite dead.

Well, this *is* curious," said Saburo, "for I distinctly heard the eel grunt." Then he stopped, scratched his head and thought: "No, I know what it was. The eel landed on the boar and the boar grunted. That's more like it. Then the eel died because he was out of water and the boar died of fright." And that is just what had happened. The eel had gone sailing through the air, turning end over end, and had finally landed with a big thump right on the back of the sleeping boar. Now boars, even though they are fierce, are very sensitive. The surprise had been just too much for its nerves.

"Oh, what luck!" said Saburo to himself. "Both eels and boars are delicious. Oh, what a feast I'll have!" Then he stopped and wondered: "How on earth can I get the boar home though?" He scratched his head. "I guess I'll have to make something to carry that big boar with. Here're some vines. I'll take some of these and use them to strap the boar onto my back and that way I can take him home."

So he pulled at the vines, but no sooner had he taken hold of one than it came loose and he saw that it had wild yams on the end. "Oh, how wonderful," said Saburo, "wild yams. How delicious they will be!" Usually wild yams are hard to pull from the ground, but today they came loose as easy as anything.

Saburo said: "Now I have an eel and a boar and lots of wild yams, but I'll have to make something to carry the yams in. Here are some reeds. I'll use these." So he set to work picking reeds. He would grasp a thick top and pull violently; then they would come loose. He pulled one and it squawked once and then lay still in his fist.

What's this?" wondered Saburo. "A reed with feathers?" But it wasn't, it was a pheasant—a nice, plump pheasant with a lovely green and red head, brown wings, and long, long tail feathers. "Well, what a nice bird you are," said Saburo patting its head, but the bird didn't move. In pulling he had wrung its neck. And there at his feet was a nest with thirteen big shiny eggs in it.

"Oh, thirteen must be my lucky number today," said Saburo. "Here I have a boar, an eel, lots of yams, a nice plump pheasant, and thirteen eggs! What a feast I'll have when I get home!" Then he stopped. "But how to get them home I wonder," he said.

He thought and thought and thought about this big problem. There really seemed to be much more than one man could ever hope to carry. But he was determined not to leave any of these wonderful things behind him. Finally he took some of the reeds

and wove a basket with them. He wove it wide and deep and strong, and then he put the pheasant and the eggs in the basket, packing them carefully in moss. Then he put the boar across his back and tied it firmly with the vines. Then he tied the yams around his neck and let them hang down over his shoulders in the front. And finally, using still more of the strong vines, he tied the eel to one of his hands. When he was all finished, he was indeed a funny-looking sight, but everything was quite safe. And that's the way he went home, carrying the eel, *and* the wild boar, *and* the yams, *and* the nice plump pheasant, *and* the thirteen eggs. All the way he kept imagining the wonderful feast he would have when he got home. His mouth was watering and he felt so happy that he didn't even notice how heavy a load he was carrying.

When he reached his house, he put all the things down on the kitchen floor and then just stood there thinking about what had happened to him. The more he thought about it, the funnier it seemed to him. He began to laugh a little, at first just a few chuckles, but soon he was rolling on the floor with laughter. When he could finally talk through his laughter, he said: "I'm a pretty good eel-catcher—that I am!" And he laughed all the way through the wonderful feast he had that night.

What do you think? Don't you agree that Saburo was a pretty good eel-catcher?

The Singing Turtle

ONCE there were two brothers. One of them was very industrious. All day long he worked in the fields. He worked very hard, and he was never sullen nor unkind. He didn't particularly like to work, but his poor mother was ill and needed the little bit of money he could earn. So he worked without complaining, even when he was very tired. It was hard to get up in the morning and start working, but he did and always had a smile for his old sick mother. In the evening he was so tired he could

hardly walk home, yet he fixed her supper and tucked her in for the night before he allowed himself to sleep.

The other brother was quite different. He was very lazy. All day long, when he was supposed to be working, he lay on the grass or lazily picked flowers. And he was always sullen and often quite unkind. He didn't like to work and so he saw no reason why he should. When he needed money he'd go to his mother, and she would give him what little she could spare. But he was never satisfied and complained constantly. He slept all the time, yet he hated to get up in the morning, and he always shouted at his brother and snarled at his mother. In the evening he would come home for money and then go into town and stay half the night spending the money foolishly.

The family became poorer and poorer because, no matter how hard the industrious brother worked, the lazy brother spent their money all the faster. Finally, one spring morning, the first brother cut some firewood and said to his mother: "I'm going into town and see if I can't sell this

The Singing Turtle

wood to make some money, for we have nothing to eat for supper tonight."
The sick mother said: "I hope you can, but don't work too hard or else
you'll be sick like me." The lazy brother, who was lying on his back
asleep in the sun, said nothing, but only snored loudly. So the industrious
brother took the enormous load of firewood on his back and started for
town.

He stayed all day but he couldn't sell a single stick of the wood. He
was very discouraged and finally put the heavy wood on his back and
started home, wondering how they would eat that day. The wood was
heavy and his heart was heavier as he trudged through the forest. Finally he
came to the little forest pond where he usually ate lunch and, putting the
wood down by a tree, he sat down on a stump and began to cry.

He was a grown man and grown men don't cry very often, so he was
very sad indeed. While he was crying he suddenly heard a voice. "Why

are you crying?" the voice asked. The young man looked all around but couldn't see anyone. "You'd better blow your nose," said the voice again. But he still couldn't see anyone.

"Where are you?" he asked finally.

"Right under the nose you'd better blow," said the voice. The young man looked down, and there was a turtle floating on a piece of wood.

"Did you speak?" asked the man.

"Naturally," said the turtle, "there's no one else around. Really, you'd better blow your nose."

But turtles don't talk," said the brother.

"This one does. And what's more, I can sing too. I like singing."

"Sing?" he said.

"Blow your nose," said the turtle. After the young man had blown his nose, the turtle continued: "And I sing very beautifully too. But say, you're in trouble, aren't you?" The brother admitted that he was and finally told the turtle the whole story. After he had finished, the turtle said: "Well, you've fed me often enough, so I'll feed you now."

"I've fed you?" asked the young man.

"Sure," said the turtle, "this is where you eat your lunches, isn't it? Well, I've been eating the crumbs you've dusted off your lap afterwards. And seeing as how you've fed me, now I'll feed you."

"You mean I'm supposed to eat you?" asked the man. "I don't think I could—not after our friendly talk and all, you know."

"No, no," said the turtle impatiently. "You take me into town, and I'll sing. Then the people will pay much money."

The young man was undecided. "Can you really sing?" he asked.

The turtle only looked disgusted. "Of course I can—just listen," he said. And then he started to sing. Actually he couldn't sing very well, but a turtle that can sing at all is such an oddity that no one ever stops to think if he's singing well or not.

"That was wonderful," said the man and, picking the turtle up, started back to town with him.

The townspeople thought that the turtle was wonderful. They had never heard a turtle sing before, and after it had sung several songs they showered the turtle and the hard-working brother with coins. The young man took this money, bought food, and hurried back home with the turtle. When the mother saw the food she was very surprised. Her son told her what had happened, and the turtle nodded his head wisely from time to time. They were very happy, but just then the lazy brother showed up, and ate up all the food.

"You didn't make very much money," he complained. "If you'd give him to me I'd bring back a fortune."

"No, you wouldn't," said the industrious brother. "You'd run away with it. You can't have the turtle."

This made the lazy brother very mad and in no time at all they began to fight. The lazy brother knocked his brother down and took the turtle to town himself.

When the townspeople gathered, the wicked brother made them give him money. Then he held the turtle up in his hands and commanded: "Sing!" But the turtle wouldn't sing a note. The brother became very angry and held him by his tail. "Sing!" he shouted. But not a sound came from the turtle. Finally the brother began whipping the turtle with a switch, but it didn't hurt the turtle at all. He just drew back into his tough shell.

At first the people laughed, but when they realized that the turtle wasn't going to sing, they became angry and wanted their money back. "This is just an ordinary turtle," they said.

"No, really, it's the same turtle you heard yesterday," said the wicked brother, becoming frightened. He hit the turtle's tough shell again and shouted: "Sing, sing!" Finally he began to plead: "Please sing, please!" But the turtle wouldn't sing a note.

The people became more angry and said: "Let's give this cheat a beating the same way he's beating that poor turtle." And they began to beat the wicked brother so hard that he howled with pain, because he didn't have a hard shell to protect him, you see. They beat him right out of town.

The turtle stuck out his head and crawled back to the house where the good brother and his mother lived. "Well, that bad man is gone," he said. "He got beaten and chased away. He'll never dare come back."

The mother and brother thought they ought to feel sorry, but actually they were relieved, and soon all three were laughing together.

Then the turtle looked shyly around the edge of its shell and said: "May I live with you? The other turtles think I'm a bit odd because I can talk and sing. I'm more at home with humans. I can make money for you."

"Oh, please do stay," said the mother and the good brother. "Whether you can make money or not, we like you."

Thus it was that the turtle stayed and lived with them. He often sang in the town, and the three of them lived very happily on the money the townspeople gave to hear his singing.

Kintaro's Adventures

ONCE there was a woodcutter and his wife living at the foot of a wild mountain called Ashigara. This woodcutter had once been a noble warrior and had lived in splendor in Kyoto, which was then the capital of Japan, but his enemies had become so strong that he finally had to flee with his wife into the mountains in order to save his life.

Soon after they came to live in the mountains the woodcutter's wife gave birth to a healthy, lively baby boy. The woodcutter was so happy that he named the baby Kintaro, which means "Golden Boy," saying that

43

his baby son was more precious than all the gold there was in Kyoto. His mother took one of her favorite jewels and hung it about the baby's neck. The jewel was made of a piece of red coral. Then she prayed: "Please help this baby boy to grow up to be a good man, a strong and healthy and fine man."

A few weeks after Kintaro was born, his father went far into the mountains one day to cut wood. His mother put the baby Kintaro in his crib to sleep while she went down to the mountain stream to wash some clothes. Suddenly, as she washed, she heard Kintaro crying loudly. "What can be the matter?" she said. And when she turned to look toward the cabin, she saw a terrible thing.

A huge bear suddenly came running out of the cabin, carrying the crying baby in his arms. Holding the baby tightly, but gently, the bear went running with it toward the mountains.

"Help! Help!" Kintaro's mother screamed with all her might. And she went running straight toward the bear.

When the bear saw the angry mother come running toward him, he turned and jumped down a steep cliff, still holding Kintaro in his arms,

and then went running down the valley toward the distant mountains.

"Help! Help!" the mother cried again. "Kintaro has been stolen!"

Just then Kintaro's father returned. Seeing what was happening, he picked up his broad ax and went running after the bear. As he ran he kept shouting out for help and other woodcutters and farmers along the way joined in the chase, running after the bear with axes and sickles and clubs.

The bear ran faster and faster, and finally he reached a deep, deep ravine with a rushing river in it. The only way across the ravine was a long, narrow log The bear ran nimbly

across this log; then he stopped and picked the log up and threw it down in the river.

Then the people who were running after the bear couldn't get across. They stood screaming on one side of the ravine, and the bear walked calmly on to his home, carrying Kintaro with him.

The bear's house was a cave deep in the mountain. There in the cave the mother bear was crying because her baby cub had died right after he was born. Father Bear came into the cave and said: "Look! I've brought a baby back for you!"

"Oh! what a darling!" Mother Bear said, taking Kintaro happily in her arms. She was so happy to have a baby to love again, and she took very, very good care of Kintaro, so that day by day he grew bigger and stronger.

Father Bear was the King of the Forest. All the animals of the forest came often to the cave with presents of berries, fruits, nuts, and honey.

Each time, Father Bear would bring Kintaro out to show him to the other animals. He would say very proudly: "Look! Isn't he a handsome, healthy boy! Someday this boy will take my place as King of the Forest."

Thus Mother and Father Bear cherished their new son. Mother Bear fed Kintaro on bear's milk, and Father Bear taught him how to wrestle. By the time he was five, Kintaro could beat all the other animals at wrestling. He won easily from the monkey, and the fox, and the badger.

They all liked him so much that they helped and taught him everything that they could do.

After a few months of hard practice Kintaro learned from Uncle Deer how to make great leaps across the ground. And he could climb any steep cliff as easily as the mountain goat, leap wide rivers, run as fast as the rabbit, swim like the otter, and even see in the dark like an owl.

When Kintaro was about eight years old, Father Bear, the King of the Forest, became very sick. Kintaro was very worried and went all over the forest to gather fruit and berries for Father Bear. But nothing did any good and Father Bear got sicker and sicker.

One day when Kintaro was at home in the cave taking care of Father Bear, a fierce, ugly wolf stuck his head in the entrance. He had come with many of his friends and servants. He glared in at the poor, sick bear and said: "Hey! you've become old and weak! You're no good any more. From now on I'm going to be king of this forest. Come, tell everyone that I'm their new king!"

The sick bear raised his head and looked at the wolf. "A mean thing like you can never become king," he said.

"All right, then," said the wolf. "I'll wrestle you, and if I win, then you'll have to admit that I'm the new king."

Father Bear got out of bed, ready to wrestle the wolf. But Kintaro

said: "You're too sick, Father Bear. Please let me wrestle the wolf in your place."

"No, no," said Father Bear. "I'm still King and I can still whip such an insolent wolf."

So the bear and the wolf started wrestling. The bear quickly caught the the wolf in his strong arms and lifted him high over his head. "Now!" roared the bear, "how do you like this. If you don't give up, I'll throw you into the bottom of that ravine."

But just then the wolf's friends and servants all jumped into the fight too. They forced the bear to the ground and he couldn't get up, no matter how much strength he had.

"Oh, you cowards!" cried Kintaro. And he jumped into the fight too. Letting fly with his fists, he beat up one wolf after another, until they all went running away into the forest, with their leader running the fastest of all.

"Thank you very much for saving me, Kintaro," said Father Bear. "You did very well. From today on, I make you King of the Forest. You must rule all the other animals justly and wisely and protect them from the wolves." And with these words Father Bear rolled over and died.

Thus Kintaro became King of the Forest.

And what had been happening back at Kintaro's real home all this time? His parents had searched for Kintaro for a long time, but they could never find him and finally gave him up for lost. A little while later, a girl baby was born to them. They named the baby Misuzu, and one day, when she was just six years old, her mother called her to her side and gave her a jewel made of white coral to hang around her neck.

"Listen to me very carefully," said her mother, "and I'll tell you something you must never forget. Before you were born, you had a brother named Kintaro, but he was stolen away by the bears."

"A brother!" said Misuzu. "Oh, how I should like to meet him!"

"Perhaps you shall someday," said her mother. "If he is still alive, he should be wearing a coral jewel around his neck. It is just like yours, except red instead of white, and that way you'll be able to recognize him if you should ever see him."

One day a few days later, Misuzu went up on the mountain to pick some berries. But she couldn't find any good ones and kept walking and walking until at last she was far into the forest where she had never been before. All at once she saw a beautiful waterfall. And there in the pool at the bottom of the falls she saw a boy about eight years old playing with a bear and a monkey and some other animals. She looked

and looked, and suddenly she saw the boy was wearing a red coral jewel around his neck.

"Oh, it's my brother—it's Kintaro!" she cried. So she began shouting down to the boy: "Kintaro! Kintaro!"

Kintaro, now King of the Forest, was surprised to hear a human voice. It was a sound he couldn't remember ever having heard before. And he looked up toward the top of the cliff where Misuzu was. But he couldn't understand human speech at all and so could only look up at her, wondering what she was saying.

Then, all of a sudden, something made a rustling sound behind Misuzu. Just as she looked around, a wolf jumped out and grabbed her.

"Help! Help!" she cried, as the wolf started to carry her away.

"Oh, how terrible!" cried the monkey to Kintaro. "That's the little girl who lives at the foot of the mountain. We must save her from the wolf!"

So Kintaro and the monkey and all the other animals climbed quickly up the cliff and began running after the wolf.

The wolf, still carrying little Misuzu, ran across a log bridge over a deep ravine and was rushing away into the mountains.

"Stop! Stop!" they yelled after him.

The monkey reached the log bridge first and started to run across it. But just then the wolf grabbed a hornets' nest from a tree and threw it at the monkey. Hundreds of buzzing hornets flew at the poor monkey, and he was so surprised that he slipped right off the log and tumbled down into the rushing river, head over heels.

"Help! Help!" the monkey cried. He was a bad swimmer and was being swept away by the rushing torrent.

Kintaro didn't know what to do. Should he keep running after the wolf who was running away with the little girl, or should he stop and

save the monkey? Finally he said to himself: "I'll save the monkey first, because he's my good friend, and then I'll save the little girl."

He dived quickly into the stream and went swimming as fast as he could after the poor monkey. It was a terrible struggle, but Kintaro finally caught hold of the monkey and barely managed to pull him out onto a bank.

When they climbed out of the ravine, they couldn't see the wolf and the little girl anywhere. "What a shame!" said Kintaro. "In a minute we could have saved her." So he

walked sadly back along the log bridge, and there he found a white coral necklace.

"The little girl must have dropped it," he said to the monkey. "Look, it's just like mine except that it's white instead of red."

"Oh," said the monkey, "that little girl must be your sister. She had a necklace just like yours, and she looked very much like you."

This made Kintaro want to save the little girl all the more. So he called a big eagle and told him: "Fly away and see if you can find the little girl."

The eagle flew up high into the sky and went whirling away. Presently he returned and told Kintaro: "The wolves have a castle over beyond the third mountain. They've locked the little girl in a tower at the top of the castle."

"All right then," said Kintaro, "let's go save her."

So Kintaro started for the wolves' castle. The bear and the wild boar and the lion and the monkey and all the other animals of the forest went with him. The eagle flew in front of them, showing them the way.

Suddenly the great eagle came flying to Kintaro and said: "Quick! Quick! There's a forest fire and if we don't put it out right away, all the trees will be burned down."

Kintaro hurried over to the general of the wolves and said to him: "Quick! If we don't put out this forest fire, all the forest will be destroyed. You must come and help us."

"All right," said the wolf general. "Everybody follow me to the river, where we'll all wet our bodies."

So they all went to the river and jumped in. When their fur was completely wet, they climbed out of the river and ran and rolled on the grass in the path of the fire. By thus wetting the grass they hoped to keep the fire from spreading.

While the animals were wetting the grass some woodcutters came running up from the lowlands. The leader of the woodcutters was Kintaro's father. He and the other woodcutters cut down the trees in the path of the fire, and thus at last the forest fire was put out. Kintaro and his followers, and the wolves as well, breathed great sighs of relief. Just then Misuzu came running out of the wolves' castle.

"Father! How glad I am that you've come! That little boy there is my brother, Kintaro. Look! isn't he wearing a red coral necklace just like my white one? He's become the King of the Forest. Let's hurry over and talk to him."

Misuzu led her father over to where Kintaro was. But Kintaro couldn't understand human speech. So by gestures Misuzu persuaded Kintaro to come home with them. It was now ten years since Kintaro had been kidnapped from his home by the bear. But Misuzu gave him lessons every day, and soon he learned how to talk.

So, now, whenever Kintaro and his father go to work cutting trees in the forest, Misuzu comes and brings them tea while they rest. Just today she brought them their tea there and found all Kintaro's friends waiting

to drink tea and eat rice-dumplings with them. There was the monkey, and the deer, and the wolves, and many more.

When they saw her coming, they all cried out, "Oh, goody!" And then they began a feast, there in the beautiful forest where the autumn leaves were turning scarlet.

—Retold by Genichi Kume